SAMIA RIDA

NESSIE AND ME

Published by Samia Rida.

Printed and bound by CPI Group UK Ltd, Croydon, CR0 4YY

ISBN 978-0-9927576-0-1

Chapter One

I look down at my doughy white legs and pull my socks up high.
All my clothes today are new and shiny and my Mummy has cut out all the labels.
I tuck my top into my skirt and like how it holds me.
The material is tight and my belly is round as I look down at it.
I look in the mirror and see my face, my two ponytails to each side of my ears that my mother did earlier and my eyes big and looking back at me.
I do not mind looking at myself when I am alone like this.
It is when I am next to others that I do not like it.

I run down the stairs to show my Mummy and Daddy how the clothes they have bought me look.
The stairs creak and thud as I place my weight on them.
Mummy is washing up at the sink and Daddy is reading the paper when I come down.
'*Mummy,*' I say, to get her to look at me.
Her yellow hair is in a whirl at the bottom of her neck and her body is still apart from her arms moving to wash the breakfast plates.

She doesn't turn around when I call her name.
'*Remember what Annie taught you about saying that word, M-u-m-m-y,*' she says, again hardly moving.
I say it again to try to please her but by now she has turned around and is looking at me.
Her eyes are wet and her smile is frozen and it is

confusing for me to try to see what she thinks or feels.
My Daddy looks too now.
'*Well aren't you beautiful*?' he says and pulls me towards him for a cuddle.
He blows into my neck and I giggle.
I catch my mother's face again mid-giggle, she looks far away.

On the way to tennis we drive past Dunkin' Donuts and I really want one.
My mother says no and her and Daddy start to argue about it.
I want one so badly that I start to cry and scream.
I want to taste the soft dough and then the cold thick custard.
I want two or three.
I want them more than anything.
When I scream for long enough they park the car and my father goes to get me one while my mother stays in the car.
He slams the car door hard and my mother puts her face in her hands for a moment.
When she looks up again she watches him go into the shop.
I can see in the mirror that her cheek has red blotches that have come out on it.
She doesn't talk and after a bit looks straight ahead of her.
I wait and all I can think of is about the sugar on my lips and the cream in my mouth.
I sit silently and still, waiting.
I feel my mother's eyes on me through the car mirror.
I think of the sugar, small and hard on my lips and licking it off after every bite.
'*It's not good for you to eat so many donuts, Lisa,*' she says.
I think of the dough, soft as my teeth bite through it.
'*Lisa, did you hear me?*'

The cream, cold and thick.
'*I'm trying to help you here, Lisa.*'
I hope my Daddy gets me two, or three, three would be better.
'*If you want the other kids at school to...*' my mother starts to say.
She doesn't finish her sentence as my father re-enters the car.
He has two donuts for me and I grab them eagerly.
My mother keeps her head fixed forward as she continues the drive to tennis.
All is silent but the sound of the paper bag the donuts come in and my mouth as it chews and swallows.
Once I finish the second donut it is harder for me to not think about how awful it is to be in this car with these two people.

Chapter Three

I arrive at tennis and in my group all the children are half my size and age.
One of the girls whose entire outfit is pink and has shiny lips asks her mother why I am there and her mother tells her to shhh.
My own mother is looking down at her shoes and my Daddy looks still like a stone.
The teacher feeds the ball to me with a big smile on his face.
His eyes do not match his smile.
I see this a lot in adults.
I try to hit the ball back.
To make my mum proud.
But my hand feels like it has only thick thumbs on it and the donuts have made me want for only the television and my cartoons.
My sofa is soft and has a dip in it where I always sit.
I like to bounce there as I sit.
My favourite is to sit there with a bowl of sausages and watch Tom and Jerry.
I laugh and laugh.
As I think of this the tennis ball hits my head and my mother shouts at me to pay attention.
It is then that I start screaming and let myself fall to the ground.
I hate coming to this place. I hate the children who talk to each other and not to me.
I hate the way I feel like a big fat giant as I stand next to all the pretty girls in pretty skirts with yellow hair and mean eyes.

I hate the way my Mummy and Daddy look so tight and serious.
They look like they hate this place as much as I do but still they want me to come every week.
My skirt is up and I am kicking and screaming and several people including my Mummy and Daddy run to me.
They have done this so many times before that they jump into action, my Daddy holding me across my arms and chest and my Mummy holding my ankles together as I kick and fight.
I am held tightly until I run out of energy to kick and move anymore.
Everyone stares and I see the parents of the other children talking to each other.
My Mummy shouts at my Daddy for giving me the donuts.
My Daddy holds my head into his chest and kisses me.
My face is wet with tears it seems.

The drive home is more silence.
The relief my fit brought is slowly being taken from me.
I feel something building again.
I want more donuts.

Chapter Four

This morning I am being taught at home and then in the afternoon I will go to school.
Melissa arrives to teach me. She is cold and doesn't look at me at all. She moves like a robot through my class and I do my best to please her.
After the class I am taken to the kitchen where Crystal gives me my lunch.
Crystal talks and talks and laughs and laughs and works and works.
And I eat and suck and lick my spaghetti bolognese and ask for more cheese, more cheese, more cheese.
After is jelly, it is wobbly and slips down my throat before I can even taste it and I want seconds and thirds and Crystal laughs and works around me.
When the taxi arrives to take me to school I feel my head, like something is pushing from the inside into my forehead.
It is the same driver as always but he never talks to me.
I look out of the window as we drive and I long for the moments when I see my Daddy, and no one else is around and he is relaxed and hugs me and laughs with me.
Annie meets me from the car and takes me to my classroom where all the children and chairs and tables are too small for me.
I feel like a giant again and imagine picking up the children like King Kong does.
Annie comes to work with me.
She asks me why I am sad today and I tell her I am lonely and I am ugly and she tells me not to be silly.

I want to say that I am not being silly and that it is all true but a lot of the time I've noticed that adults don't want to be told what is true and you can tell them and tell them and they'll still try to say that it isn't so.

When I get home I watch television and eat sausages on my lap.

Mummy is out at a dinner and Daddy seems like although his body is here, his mind is somewhere else. Somewhere far far away.

When it is bedtime he holds my hand to take me up to bed. He makes silly jokes while I brush my teeth and makes me laugh and spit out my toothpaste.

We snuggle in my bed and I am allowed with my Daddy to read whatever book I like. I chose my favourite one about the Loch Ness Monster and Daddy tells me about his father in Scotland and how we will visit there one day together.

Right when it is time to say goodnight I pluck up all my courage, '*Daddy?*'

'*Yes, darling?*' he says.

'*I don't want to do tennis anymore, Daddy.*'

He looks at me, deep into me. I love the way his look feels and I am warm and safe.

He stays like this for quite a long time and then, finally, he replies.

'*Okay, you don't want to go... you won't go.*' He kisses my forehead.

'*Daddy?*' I say.

'*Yes, darling?*'

'*I want to do swimming classes, for when we go to see the Loch Ness Monster, so I can go in and meet her.*'
Again, he pauses. It's starting to get on my nerves a bit now until his reply is:
'*Swimming,*' he says with a smile. '*Swimming it is.*'

Chapter Five

Daddy is taking me to school this morning. It is Friday and I go to school in the morning only. They call it inclusion.
We wait in the playground for my teacher Annie to come and get me. All the mothers huddle and talk and Daddy stands alone with me.
He seems uneasy and is looking around a lot.
He takes a big inhale before walking up to a group of mothers.
'*Hello,*' he says.
They seem shocked to be approached. I stand slightly behind him and watch the children play together before the other teacher rings the bell for them to line up.
I dread this bell. It is so loud it makes my body shake and jump.
'*I just wondered if any of you were able to recommend a good swimming teacher?*'
There is a moment of silence before a woman with a kind face comes forward to talk to my Daddy.
He puts a number in his phone and then Annie arrives.

He kisses me and tells me he loves me before I go in with Annie.
As Annie walks me in she says that my Daddy is handsome and that I am lucky to have such a Daddy.

I carry his kiss and words like a warm snugly cardigan around me all morning.
And I think of what I will say when I first meet Nessie and how I will stroke her long neck.

Annie tells me it is good to daydream.
All the adults I know seem to say different things about what is good or bad.

Chapter Six

When we get to the swimming pool it is noisy. The room is echoey and splashy and there are squeals and laughter. I feel my head start to spin and my Daddy gets very still again.
Everywhere there are children.
Screaming and splashing and jumping and playing.
I start to feel like my head is spinning and it is all very frightening.

He crouches down and holds me by both shoulders and looks me in my eyes.
'*Lisa, Lisa, look at me.*'
I try to force myself to focus and force my eyes to look into his eyes.
'*Lisa, it's going to get quieter here very soon. The last class must be overrunning. I'm sorry, darling. Shall we go out and come in again in a few minutes once they have gone?*'
I do not know what to say or do so I just stand very still and keep looking in my Daddy's eyes.
I see behind him a line of children slowly making their way out of the pool and into the changing rooms.
All of a sudden the water becomes still.
I can just see someone swimming below the surface up and down the length of the pool.
When the person swims the water hardly splashes at all.

My father and I sit on the side and I feel my body soften slowly as the big room becomes quiet.
I let out a sigh and let the stillness wash over me.

I know we are waiting for my teacher Alan.
We are silent as we wait but it is not the kind of silence I have with my Mummy.
With my Mummy the silence hurts my head, it feels like the room gets smaller and the walls are tight against me.
When it is silent with my Mummy I feel like having one of my fits and like I can't breathe and can't bear how I am feeling.

With my Daddy it is different. The silence is comfy, like a soft bed.
I rest my head on his shoulder as we wait and he puts his arm around me.
I know I will never get married like other girls but if I were to I would want to marry my Daddy.

The person swimming slowly surfaces from the water and up the steps of the pool.
His skin is black and shiny and he has a bit of a belly over his shorts.
He has a big smile as he walks towards us and his teeth are white against his face.
My father stands to meet him.
'*Hello,*' the man says holding his hand out to me, '*you must be Lisa.*'
'*Hello,*' I say.

'*Hi, nice to meet you,*' he says after to my Daddy.
'*You too, um, as it's Lisa's first time, as I mentioned on the phone, I think we should...*'

‘*Mr Lewis, I think we're going to do fine. Why don't you stay on the side here and watch the first class.*’
My father sits as he is told.

My teacher holds my hand and walks towards the pool with me.
‘*My name is Alan. Now I must warn you, we are going to have a lot of fun together. Are you ready?*’
‘*Yes,*’ I say and I can feel my smile tickling my face and bursting to come out.
‘*Now, I want you to sit here a moment with your feet dangling in the water and promise you won't get in without me.*’
‘*I won't.*’
I settle myself on the side and feel the coldness of the water on my feet and halfway up my legs.
All of a sudden Alan runs towards the water, makes himself into a ball and splashes into the pool.
Water is all over me, my hair, my head, my face and my body.
My father looks worried and stands.
I see Alan nearing the top of the pool and then breaking out through the water.
I see his teeth white and his big smile.
And I am laughing and wet as he approaches me with his arms out.
I jump into the pool.
And he catches me.

Chapter Seven

All the way home we talk and laugh.
My hair is still a little wet and loose and my skin feels shiny and clean.
I am telling my Daddy all the things Alan taught me and how I told him I am going to see Nessie and want to be able to swim with her.
I tell my Daddy that Alan asked when it is we are visiting Nessie and I decide that it is in the summer.
Daddy starts to say he's not sure, not sure if we can go that soon.

When we get home everything changes.
Mummy is there and she hangs up the phone the minute we get in.
She is angry and I am told to go to my room.
I hear shouting.
But this time instead of the usual feeling building in me I go to my bookcase.
I get Nessie down and I look at her.
I imagine easily the feeling of the water as I go into the Loch.
And Nessie smiling at me as I cuddle her neck and climb onto her back.
And I feel okay.
I feel okay.
I feel okay.

Chapter Eight

When I come down to breakfast only my Mummy is there.
She is putting cereal into a bowl and adding milk for me before she brings it to me at the table.
She is wearing heels and perfume and make up and her face is frozen.
I try to disappear as I sit there.
I feel like the house is holding its breath.

'*Lisa, you won't be going swimming again. Your Daddy and I have talked and you are to keep going to tennis.*'
Something in me snaps and before I know it I am kicking and screaming and lashing and breaking.
My bowl is smashing on the floor and there are Rice Krispies and milk everywhere.
I want to hurt her and hurt myself, I want to whack myself against things and I want the pain to bring me relief.
I want to squash and smash.

'*I hate you, I hate you, I hate you!*' I am screaming now.
I am spitting and sobbing and lashing.
And my Mummy is shouting '*I can't take this anymore. I'm going to put you in a home. I can't take any more of this.*'
The door goes and my Mummy holds my face in both her hands and puts her face close to mine.
'*Please stop it, Lisa, please. Please stop it Lisa, I beg you. I beg you, Lisa. Stop it. Stop it.*'
And she is crying, sobbing, tears and tears and saliva

coming out of her mouth and she is near and soft and I can smell her perfume and see the foundation in the creases of the lines around her face.

I feel and smell her breath and my heart is full of love.

There is some milk on her face and cereal on her top.

Around us my chair is on its side and the bowl is broken around the floor.

I rest my forehead on hers and for a moment she softens into me and me into her.

And then quickly, she freezes and gets up and I feel like my heart is aching unbearably.

Like a proper feeling of pain in my heart.

'*Melissa is here*.' she says and walks off to the door.

Chapter Nine

Daddy has not been home for days now.
The only person who brings me any joy is gone.
I do not know why or where and every day is impossible to get through.
In the evenings I hear Mummy on the phone.
Sometimes she is crying and sometimes she is whispering.
Last night I heard her saying that she hears other parents upset that their children are growing up and will one day leave and that she envies them.
That her child will always need looking after.
How can this happen to her.
What has she done to deserve this.
I think I must be really bad to make her feel this way.
I think that Daddy has gone.
And that I should too.
I wonder how long it will take me to get to the Loch and if perhaps I can live with Nessie.

After my Mummy puts me to bed and goes downstairs I quietly get ready.
I pack two pairs of track pants and two jumpers; pants, socks and my Nessie book in my big bag.
I have two five pounds, three two pound coins, two pound coins and a fifty pence which I put in my pocket.
My heart feels heavy, literally as if it is heavy, weighted, and I am finding it hard to get the energy to leave.

My bed is calling me, soft and warm and I wish for the duvet to be totally over my head.

I miss my Daddy and long for him to be in and my Mummy to be out.
I decide to lie down on my bed and imagine my father there with me.
His chest next to mine, and the feeling of his hair through his t-shirt as I rest my head on his chest.
The feel of his voice on my ear as he reads the book about Nessie.
His breath lifting and dropping and my head with it.
And as I imagine this I fall asleep.

Chapter Ten

When I wake up in the morning Mummy is downstairs.
She is quiet and still and her face is bare.
Her make up is all over the table but none is on her face yet.

'*Good morning, Mummy*,' I say. '*Good morning darling*,' she says.
There is the smell of cigarettes in the house and two wine glasses by the side of the sink.

Mummy gets up and puts my cereal in a bowl and adds milk.
As I eat my cereal she puts on her make up.
My Mummy doesn't eat breakfast and every few minutes she blows on her coffee before sipping it.

I am thinking about when I can start my journey to the Loch and if there is anything else I should pack.
I decide once Mummy has gone to work I should take some food from the kitchen and put it in my bag.

I will have to find a time when no one is around.

When a key goes in the lock of the front door Mummy looks worried.
I am finishing the last few bits of my cereal and waiting to drink the sweet milk that is always left in the bowl.

Daddy walks in. He kisses me and his face prickles me on my cheeks.

He then kisses Mummy. She looks like a statue.
And then he speaks, '*I will be taking Lisa to her swimming class after school today*,' he says.
Mummy's eyes go all watery as she stands up.
She walks up to Daddy and he puts his arms around her.
He is like a bear I think, and he completely swallows Mummy up when he cuddles her.
They stay like that for a while and I can hear, every now and then, my Mummy sobbing.
I drink my milk from the bowl and it is the best it's ever tasted.

Chapter Eleven

We get to the pool and this time it is quieter.
Again Alan is swimming up and down the pool.
It is beautiful to watch him.
He looks as though he belongs in the water.

I am excited to feel the water on my legs and arms and face and hair.
I remember how I felt when I was with Alan last time and want to feel that again.

My father and I sit in silence.
He is so big next to me and I lean my head on his shoulder and he strokes my hair.

I relax watching Alan go back and forth along the pool and listening to the echoey room.

After a while I let my eyes close.
I imagine Nessie smiling at me.
I imagine looking into her eyes and her eyes match her smile.
They are kind and I feel safe when I look into them.

'*How is my favourite girl?*' I hear. And I smile before opening my eyes.
'*I have been looking forward to seeing you all day.*'
I look at my Daddy and he is smiling too.

Alan takes my hand and I sit on the side of the pool and dangle my feet and legs in the water.

We start the class with him asking me to lie in the water on my back.
He keeps telling me to relax my body, totally relax my body.
I keep trying to do as he asks but he keeps saying it.
'*Relax, Lisa, totally relax your body.*'
I close my eyes and cannot stop my mouth from smiling.
This is the best feeling ever.

On the way home I am giggling and we stop for chicken and chips at my favourite place.
I ask Daddy if he saw me floating, and if he saw me when I sat on Alan's back and he swam and he said that it looked like magic when we did that, like I was sitting and moving in the water without moving my arms or legs.
And I am so happy.

Chapter Twelve

When we get home Mummy is there.
I think maybe I can tell her about my swimming class.
That things can be good now. That we can all be happy.
That life can start to change.
She doesn't say hello even though we have walked in the door and she must hear us.
I am not sure what to do so go to my room and get my Nessie book out.
I tell Nessie about my class with Alan and how I ride on his back and maybe, when we meet I can ride on hers.

I hear shouting from downstairs. My Mummy is crying. She is saying to Daddy that she finds me ugly and disgusting, that I have shattered her life. That all her dreams of the future are gone. That she knows he can't bear to hear this but this is how she feels and she must be heard.
I try to remember how it felt when Alan held me in the water and I was floating.
I try to remember the food I had with my Daddy and how happy I was.
But all I can think is if my Mummy hates me I want to die.
And Nessie or Alan or Daddy can't fix that.

Then I hear something I have never heard before. Daddy is shouting. He is shouting at my Mummy that she is shell fish. I wonder why he is saying that. He says that she is ugly, her hatred is ugly, her rejection of Lisa is ugly, that she is not a mother and she shouldn't have been blessed with me and that he wants to leave.

And then I feel it happening again. My heart is beating fast and my heart and head are hurting. But this time I can't breath also. All I can think of is how I don't want to be in this house without my Daddy. And how it was when he left before. And now I can't see properly. And I am trying to cry out *Daddy*, *Daddy*, but I can't get it to happen. And the room is spinning and Daddy's voice is sounding funny, and Mummy cries. And then it all goes black.

Chapter Thirteen

I wake up and I am in a strange room.
It is very busy outside my room and there are doctors and nurses passing all the time.
I do not know how I got here or why I am here.
I rub my eyes and try to remember.
My body feels stiff and I stretch and yawn.

When my mother walks in to the room I am in, with her eyes red, I remember everything that happened and I feel something I have never felt before.
It builds from my belly upwards.
'I find her ugly and disgusting.'
I remember.
This feeling in my belly, travelling upwards, is so strong it frightens me.
'She has shattered my life.'
She comes towards me, she is talking, crying, her arms out.
I am looking back at her.
I know before I would have wanted to put my arms out too, I would have been so happy, I would have held on to this moment where my mother loves me.
I don't know what has happened.
As she gets nearer I spit, in her face.
It hits her in between her left eye and her nose.
It dribbles down her face.
She is so still and so am I and now I am frightened.
She slaps me round my face and then runs out.
And I am surprised that I start laughing.
I start laughing and laughing and laughing.

Laughing until tears come out of my eyes and my belly hurts.

My Daddy arrives a few minutes later and asks me why I have a red cheek.
I tell him that I spat at Mummy and then she slapped me.
He starts walking back and forth in the small room.
'*She did what…?*'
'*It doesn't matter, Daddy.*'
'*It bloody does matter.*'
'*It doesn't, Daddy. You don't understand, I don't care anymore. I don't care if Mummy doesn't love me.*'
'*She does love you, Lisa.*'
'*Daddy, it's okay,*' I tell him. '*It's okay.*'
After I say this he sits on my bed and hugs me.
He starts crying into my shoulder and I do what he does to me when I am sad.
I stroke his hair.
'*It's okay, Daddy. It's okay.*'
He starts laughing and so do I.
'*Lisa,*' he says looking at me with his eyes creased and smiling and red.
'*Yes, Daddy?*'
'*I think it's time we went to see Nessie.*'
'*Hurray!!!*' I yell.
So loudly that a few of the nurses look in from outside my room.

Chapter Fourteen

'Ok, so tickets, I know summer is nearly here but it's going to rain probably most of the time so we need waterproofs, wellies, fleeces, have you got your underwear, I guess you need...bring them all, I'm not sure how and where we'll wash them but....'
My Daddy keeps talking and talking.
Not really to me. Just talking.
I am not sure if I am feeling very good.
I have not seen my mother for three weeks.
When I finished school yesterday my Daddy told them I wouldn't be back now before they break up for summer.
I am sitting on my bed and there are piles of clothes around me.
And Daddy is talking and talking and talking.
It is like I feel something bad is about to happen but I don't know what.
I remember Annie telling me I need structure.
I asked her what structure is and she said it is when you know what is happening and at what time.
I think that maybe if I know what is happening and at what time it will take away this feeling.
'Daddy, what time is the train?'
'Huh? One minute, Lisa. Jesus, I don't know where your mother put your winter stuff.'
I start to move my body backwards and forwards. Sometimes this helps me but my brain still feels like it is trying to find something. And that it won't rest until it does.
'Daddy?'
He doesn't answer.

I am rocking a lot now. But it is not helping me.
'Daddy, Daddy, Daddy?'
'Yes, Lisa, please, just hold on a minute.'
He is packing now and looking for something every now and then.
In the drawer, puts something in the case, in the wardrobe, again adds something to the case, under the bed, '*not there*' he says to himself.
His movements are quick and I do not like them.
'Daddy, Daddy, Daddy, Daddy, Daddy.'
'LISA!!! For God's sake what is it?'
'What time is the train, Daddy? The train. What time is the train? The train. I need to know the time of the train Daddy.'
He stops moving and looks at me.
I am so glad he has stopped moving.
'Lisa, darling, I'm trying to find the ticket. Can you give me a minute to find it? Please, darling. Just a minute. And then I can tell you. I had it a minute ago. Your old Dad is going mad!'
'Okay Daddy, thank you Daddy.'
'Pleasure, darling.'

Daddy has just got everything we need in our case when the bell goes and the taxi is here.
He writes a note to Mummy.
She will come back to the house while we are gone he tells me.
It feels funny to know that she will be here soon.
From the taxi we go to the station.

It is busy as Daddy told me it would be and he holds me close.

I do what Annie has taught me to do.

I count to 50. And then I start again. All the way until we are in our seats in the train.

Daddy sits by me and we look out of the window.

And as the buildings go and fields and green are what I see I feel better.

I watch Daddy's eyes how they travel right to left quickly as the train moves.

He has a hair coming out of his right nostril and some gunk in his right eye.

I see his chest as it lifts and lowers with every breath.

And he has a little red vein under his left eye.

'*What are you looking at Lisa?*' he laughs.

'*I'm looking at you Daddy,*' I say.

Sometimes he laughs and I really couldn't tell you why.

Chapter Fifteen

Daddy wants to stop in Glasgow before we continue to see Nessie.
The place we are sleeping in looks down over the Botanical Gardens he tells me.
It is small and down the stairs from the street.
We eat in cafes and restaurants.
My Daddy doesn't brush my hair or put it into ponytails and I try to do it myself.
We sit in silence a lot and it feels funny that my Mummy is not here.
She calls my Daddy and speaks to me too.
She tells me to take care of myself and take care of Daddy.
She tells me she loves me.
She would never tell me that at home but now everyday she tells me she loves me.
Sometimes she cries at the end of the phone call and sometimes she doesn't.
Daddy does not speak to her for very long.

Daddy has brought his computer and on it we look and read about Nessie.
My favourite picture is her in the water with just her neck sticking out and her head.
It is one of the real ones not the silly drawings and it looks like it is evening.

I think that Nessie looks lonely, and I am sad when I think that.
Daddy says she is not seen very much as she is afraid of

people and she thinks people will be mean to her.
I want to somehow tell her that I am not one of those people.
I am not mean.
And I know what it feels like when people are mean so I would never do that.
I wonder if we could be best friends.
And when we are together the people wouldn't be mean as we are two.

I tell my Daddy about this and he says not to worry about mean people.
They are unhappy.
I think of the girls at my school and I wonder how they can be unhappy.
They are pretty and laugh and have friends.
They don't look unhappy to me.

In one of the restaurants a couple sit near us.
They are kissing a lot and my Daddy looks over at them many times.
They look like they don't see anyone but each other.
My Daddy looks funny when he looks at them.

I look from them to my Daddy and them to my Daddy.
After a while of us not talking I speak to my Daddy so he will turn to me.
When he does I hold his face and I give him a big kiss on the lips like I see the woman is doing to the man.
He jumps back from me.

He asks me what I am doing and I tell him I am doing what that woman is doing to that man.
He tells me he is my Daddy and I should not do that with my Daddy.
He is laughing and again I do not know what is funny.
He says when I have a boyfriend I will do that with him.
I do not know why he is talking about when I will have a boyfriend when he knows that I will never have a boyfriend and I know that I will never have a boyfriend.

I remember this day as the day my tummy started hurting.
A dull ache.

Chapter Sixteen

When I wake up I feel wet all down my legs.
I can hear my Daddy snoring and some light comes through the gap in the curtain.
I am too sleepy still to move.
I am wondering if I have peed myself.
And how I am going to tell Daddy if I have.

My legs are stuck together a little by the wetness.
'Daddy?'
He snores.
'Daddy?'
Snore, snore, snore, snore.

I put the light on by the side of my bed and it is now that I see blood all over my hand.
I stare at the blood.
I do not know what to do.
I think maybe I am dying.

'Daddy, Daddy, Daddy.'
'What is it Lisa? Can you sleep a bit more? Daddy's tired.'
'Daddy, Daddy, Daddy.'
'Oh God, Lisa. What is it?'
'I'm bleeding, Daddy. There's blood. On my hand from my legs.'

Daddy now jumps up out of his bed and rushes to me.
He looks really worried and this makes me feel even more scared.

'Daddy, Daddy, what is it?'
'Okay, okay, Lisa. Ok keep calm. Does it hurt? Does it hurt anywhere? Where is the blood coming from? Can you show me?'
I pull the blanket off me and see the blood on the sheet, on my legs and my knickers, full of blood.
'Daddy, Daddy, I'm scared, Daddy. What is it?'
'Oh, Lisa, oh, Lisa, darling. Oh, Jesus Christ. You've started your period.'

Chapter Seventeen

I sit in the bath while Daddy runs to the shop.
He comes back with a paper bag.
He is moving very quickly and speaking to Mummy on the phone.
I can hear her down the phone, her voice sounds excited and then she sounds like she is crying.
Again.
He passes the phone to me.
'*Oh, my darling, you're turning into a woman. I should be there. I should be there with you.*'
'*It's okay, Mummy, Daddy is here.*'
'*This is a very exciting day for you, my darling. I have told Daddy what you need to do. You need to put one of the pads he's bought you in your knickers and when it gets full of blood you need to change it for another one.*'
'*Okay, Mummy.*'
I can see Daddy through the door, taking the sheets off the bed.
'*Oh, my darling Lisa, I love you. I love you so.*'
And then more crying.
I do not understand why she is crying so much.
Daddy returns and I hand the phone to him.
I am worried I will get it wet with the bath water and she is only crying mainly anyhow.
The water in the bath has gone a pink colour.
I move my feet forward and backwards in the water.
I hear Daddy telling Mummy not to worry and that he has it covered.
As I move in the water I think again of Nessie.
I imagine her sitting opposite me in the bath.

Maybe she can come home with me.
I imagine looking into her kind eyes and face.
And smiling at her as she smiles at me.
I imagine telling her I love her and her telling me she loves me.
And I imagine it feeling different from when my Mummy tells me she loves me.
When my Mummy tells me I feel worried and funny and confused.
Like she wants something and I do not know what.
But when Nessie tells me she loves me I just feel happy and warm and like it is the best feeling ever.
When I come out of the bath I feel good and clean.
Daddy has put the mattress on its side and opened windows and on the floor are the sheets with my blood on them.
He puts his arm around my shoulder and pulls me in.
'*Well, young lady, let's go and get breakfast. We are celebrating. We are celebrating you becoming a woman. I think that's what your mother told me to say anyway.*'
As we walk out of the room we get stuck in the door and giggle.
The pad feels fat between my legs and I wonder why everyone is pretending to be so damn happy about me bleeding.

Chapter Eighteen

We are back on the road now, as my Daddy likes to call it.
We have one more stop before we see Nessie and that is to see my grandad.
He lives in a house with lots and lots of old people.
He had to move there once my grandma died.
He talks funny and often my Daddy will explain to me what he has said.
The house with all the old people is in a place called Pitlochry.
It smells funny in there.
My Daddy has told me on the train journey how he remembers his Daddy being young and fit and how sad he finds it to see him old and skinny.
I don't like to think about the same happening to my Daddy.

My Grandad looks so happy when he sees us and my Daddy's eyes fill with tears.
He hugs my Daddy and then me and we sit with him.
My Daddy asks him how he is and he says how horrible it is to be old.
That the other people there are so boring and how he misses my Daddy's Mummy.
My Daddy looks so sad when he listens.
He asks Grandad what he can do, can he take him home with him to London and Grandad says no, that he has enough on his plate with Lisa.
Adults do this a lot. They talk as though I am not there.
My Daddy doesn't do this though.

He tells my Grandad that I am no trouble, in fact I am a joy and he kisses my head.

My Grandad and Daddy cry when they say goodbye to each other.
They agree we will come back after seeing Nessie.
My Daddy is quiet for ages as we walk and then wait to get on the train.
I know not to say anything.
Sometimes I wonder why life has to be so sad.
I don't even feel like seeing Nessie now.
I try to think what I can say to help him.
I think what he says to me when I am sad and decide I will say it back.
We get on the train and after a while we show our tickets to the ticket man.
My Daddy pulls some food and drinks out of his bag and puts them on the table.
'*I love you, Daddy, and I want you to be happy.*'
He looks at me with tears in his eyes and starts crying.
He just sits with his head in his hands and his body shaking.
I sit and look at him.
I put my hand on his head and stroke his hair.
I love the feeling of how the train bumps and swings.
I cuddle up to my Daddy and feel him breathing through his back.
I feel on his front that his tears have made him wet on his face and chest.
He holds my arm in his hand and squeezes me.

I say to my Daddy '*I am sorry, Daddy, that you are sad, I am sorry Grandad is sad, I am sorry Mummy is sad.*'
He looks at me and it is a surprise to me that he looks so quickly at me.
He says to me '*Enough of this horseshit. Enough of being sad. I've had enough of fucking sadness, Lisa.*'
I'm pretty sure some of those words are not allowed but I don't care.
I see something I really really love on my Daddy's face.
I kiss his wet cheeks and laugh and he laughs back.
'*I am hungry, Lisa. What about you? I am fucking hungry.*'
'*I am fucking hungry too, Daddy.*'
A woman walks past shaking her head and Daddy and me laugh and laugh.

Chapter Nineteen

When we get to Inverness it is dark and we are tired.
We get to the hotel and go and shower before we go to get some food.
The rain is so so loud outside the window and I sit and look out while Daddy is showering and getting dressed.
I cannot believe that we are going to see Nessie soon.
My Mummy has not been calling so often.
I think about my school and all the children there.
How none of them talk to me.
How they whisper to each other when they are around me.
I think of Alan, my lovely swimming teacher and his white teeth and big, big smile.
I think of my Grandad. Alone in his chair with all those old smelly people.
I think of my Daddy and his sadness.
I don't know what I can do about all this sadness.

'*Lovely Lisa, meter maid, where would I be without you. Give us a drink and make me think of you.*'
I start giggling as I hear my Daddy's voice getting closer.
I smell the soap from his shower before I feel him walking nearer to me.
I do not know if he is going to tickle me or blow a raspberry on my neck and I wriggle and giggle as I wait to see.
When he gets nearer he stops and looks at me.
'*So, Lisa, we are here darling.*'
'*I know, Daddy.*'
'*Are you excited?*'

'Yeah, I guess.'

He sits down with me

'You don't sound very excited.'

'I'm thinking about Mummy and Grandad and you and school.'

'There's something about this place that makes that happen.'

'I worry about the sadness, Daddy. Everyone is so sad.'

'Lisa, darling, this is for you. This experience is for you. Let go of everyone's sadness. This is yours.'

I think about that. Think about if that is possible.

I don't know if it is but I know I am going to try.

I do not know what it would feel like not to think about my Mummy and Daddy's sadness and how it is my fault.

'It is my fault, Daddy, the sadness. It is my fault.'

His eyes fill with tears.

'Listen to me, Lisa. Our sadness is not your fault. I have never in all my life met someone as pure and happy and wonderful as you. I would not swap you with anyone.'

'Mummy wishes I was normal Daddy. I wish I was normal Daddy.'

'What is normal Lisa? Is Nessie normal? We don't even know what normal is. We decide what it is and then try to make everything fit in with whatever we have decided is normal. Fuck normal.'

'Daddy, I don't think you are meant to say that word.'

'Sorry, Lisa.' he is laughing.

Again the laughing. Why? You tell me.

I like it though.

He kisses my head.

'I am hungry, Lisa. I am bleeping hungry.'
'Daaaaaddddddd.'
He walks off laughing and clasping my hand behind him.

Chapter Twenty

I wake up early the next day, before my Daddy.
The rain is still pouring down and I lie in bed and listen to it's sound.
I pull my duvet up around me but leave my feet sticking out just as I like it.
I can hear my Daddy's breath.
Sometimes snoring and sometimes just heavy.

Today is the day I have been waiting for.
This is the day I have thought of when I am sad or when I feel scared or lonely.
Daddy was talking to me last night as we were eating.
He told me not to be disappointed if I didn't see Nessie.
That we could leave a note for her and she would come and get it once we had gone and she knew it was safe.
But I desperately want to see her.

Today feels like getting to the top of a hill only I don't want to go down the other side.
I don't even want to see over the other side which will mean going back home, back to school, back maybe even to my Mummy and away from Nessie and Scotland and hotels and my Daddy.
All these thoughts make me want to stay in bed for even longer.

I hear my Daddy's breathing change.
Before it was in a rhythm like the rain
Now it isn't.
I know he will wake soon and we will begin our journey

to Nessie.
My stomach feels funny.
My Daddy starts to stretch and yawn.
I feel him looking over towards me but I keep my eyes closed.
I do not feel ready to start the day.

After a bit he gets up and goes to the bathroom.
I hear the sound of his peeing in the toilet.
He yawns again which makes me want to laugh but instead I just keep my eyes shut tight.
He comes back into the room.
'*I know you're awake,*' he sings, laughing.
'*How do you know, Daddy?*'
'*Because you swallowed. No one swallows in their sleep.*'
'*Daaaaddddddyyy.*' I pull my pillow out and throw it at him.
He throws it back and then goes into the shower.
I take out my Nessie book one last time.
I look at her in the lake.
I must have been looking at her for a while as my Daddy comes back in having finished his shower and got dressed.
He smells nice and his eyes look tired.
'*So, Lisa, this is the day you have been waiting for.*'
'*I am scared, Daddy.*'
'*That's natural, darling.*'
'*What if she is not there? What's going to happen when we go back home. Who will look after me?*'

'*Lisa,*' he kneels down near to me. '*If she is not there she will still know that you came and that you care. We will leave her a note as we said. You will feel her there, Lisa. It is a very special place. And as for when we get home, I don't know for sure but I know and can promise you that I will never leave you, Lisa. I will never let you down. You don't have to worry.*'
He cuddles me and his jumper is so warm like a teddy.
I feel a little better but I am still feeling funny.
Like everything is a blank.
Like there is nothing.
It is a scary feeling.

We get a taxi from the hotel to the Loch.
The driver talks and talks.
His voice is funny and, like with my Grandad, I can only catch every few words he says.
My Daddy talks with him and laughs and I am left to look out of the window.
The rain has stopped and the sky is beginning to clear.
There are blue patches in between the clouds.
I want the journey to last forever.
I don't ever want to start to come down from the top of the hill.

Chapter Twenty-One

The Loch is different to how I imagine it. Different to the pictures.
A group of people walk past us almost as soon as we arrive.
They are taking photos and talking and I feel angry that they are there.
How is Nessie going to come out if all these people are around?
There is also a family and a child throwing stones into the Loch.
I am angry with them also.

Daddy laughs when he sees my face.
He says just to wait and they will all leave.
That they are not dedicated like us.
He says just to sit it out.

We get settled.
The woman at the hotel has put a bag together for us.
It has food and blankets and waterproofs and drinks.
I help my Daddy to put it all out and we sit together.

Soon, as he says, all the people go.
And the lake becomes still.
We cuddle up.
Sometimes we talk and sometimes we don't.
We try to wait until we are really hungry to eat.
That way, Daddy says, the food tastes its best.
And as it is going to be a long day we want to make the most of all the small things that happen.

As we look at the Loch Daddy asks me how I am.
I tell him that I am scared of going home.
That I am still feeling scared of not seeing Nessie.
That I feel like Mummy is a stranger and I don't know how to be with her.
That I don't know why she doesn't love me and that I hate her for it.
That it is a Mummy's job to love her child.
And that if I was ever a Mummy I would love and love and love my child.
That I didn't want to go back to a school where everyone was normal and I wasn't.
And where everyone made me know that, every minute that I was there.
At some point within all this I start crying.
My Daddy is just looking at me and listening.
His face looks really sad as he does this.
I tell him I don't know what to want out of my life.
That I will not marry, I will not have children.
That I cannot work.
That I am ugly.
That every day feels so difficult to get through.
And that I am only happy with him, or Alan, or in my room with my book on Nessie.
And that I don't know how I can carry on living like this.
He is crying also now.
This trip has had as much crying as it has rain I think.
Just tears going down his face as he looks strongly at me.
Listening, listening, listening.
After I have said everything, everything that is in my

heart I just cry and cry and Daddy holds me and holds me.

After a long time he starts talking back.
He says that my mother is just a person, that, yes, she is my Mummy and she should be better at it, but, that basically mummies and daddies are just people.
And that she has problems.
Problems that make her not be able to love properly.
And that it is right that I am angry but I should not let her ruin my life.
He says that children are cruel and do not understand so many things.
And people are scared. Scared of things that are different. And that the fear is theirs not mine.
That I should use their behaviour to make me work harder and do better.
And that I am free, as I do not need to be one of their gang.
And that freedom is the most important thing.
And that I can have a fantastic life, and it is just beginning, and I can do anything I want to do.
And that he will always be here.
Always, and that he will support and help me achieve anything and everything I want to as long as I put my heart and soul into it also.

It sounds like a good plan to me.
And as the day starts to come to an end we sit in silence again.

I cannot believe this feeling of peace I have now.
The Loch is still and I feel like I am the Loch and the Loch is me.
I tell Daddy this and he says he knows.
He feels at one too.
At one.

We decide that maybe we should go soon.
We have not seen Nessie and I am sorry for that.
We take it in turns to take photos of each other in front of the Loch.
And then I write my letter.

Dear Nessie

I came to see you today.
I understand that maybe you want to wait until I am gone to come out.
I understand that you do not trust people to be kind to you.
I hope you are happy Nessie.
I love you.

Lisa.

We place my note on the side of the Loch and look out one last time.

I have a feeling that is new to me again.
I feel like I can do things, I can go and have my life and

who is my mother, or the children at school, to stop me. I feel like I know it will be hard for me but I will do it anyway.
I tell Daddy this and he tells me I am strong now.
I am strong.

Daddy's phone rings and it is the taxi to tell us he is waiting.
It is the same driver as before but this time he is quiet as we drive back to our hotel.
Tomorrow we will start our journey home.

Chapter Twenty-Two

Grandad will arrive in two days and there is a lot to do before his room or our new flat is ready.
There are boxes everywhere that we haven't unpacked and we can't touch any of the doors until the paint dries.
My Mummy comes by with flowers and some drinks.
Her face still looks weird when I look at it but there is something else there.
She looks like she almost likes me, or a bit of her does.
But that that is a new experience to her and strange.

She puts the items down and asks if she can do anything to help.
My Daddy says no, he's got it covered.
And my Mummy says she's on the end of the phone if he needs her.
She kisses me on the head and tells me to look after Daddy.

After some time we decide to walk along the high street and pick up the photos from Scotland and then go for some lunch.
Jerry at the café ruffles my hair when we enter and asks my dad how it's all going.
When my dad tries to pay for what we order he says no, that it's on him.
My Daddy looks like he's going to cry when Jerry says that and tries to make Jerry take the money but he won't.

We sit to eat and put the envelope with the photos in on the table.

I tell my Daddy that perhaps he should get a girlfriend soon.
He laughs and says that that is the last thing on his mind right now.
But I want him to have someone to go to dinner with and to help him with all he is doing.
I tell him he can't spend every night with a pizza and a can of beer watching TV and he laughs again and tells me not to spy on him when I should be asleep.

We take it in turns to wash our hands before opening the photos.
It is strange to go through the last few weeks all over again as we go through picture after picture.
There is us at the beginning on the train, the hotel, the restaurants, the gardens, the trains, my Grandad…
My Daddy looks at the photos and then passes them to me.
I like to watch his face as he looks at them and try to guess what is coming next.

He stops and looks very closely at one. He is holding on to it for so long that I am getting impatient. He holds it close to his face and he looks funny. I cannot read what he is thinking.
But he looks really weird. And his skin has gone very pale.
I don't even want to speak almost but cannot stop myself.
'*What is it, Daddy?*' I say. '*What is it?*'

He doesn't say anything but just looks at me as he passes the photo.
There is me standing in front of the Loch and behind me, as clear as daylight, is Nessie, smiling and kind and beautiful and proud.
I do not know what to say.
I just stare at the photo for what feels like forever.

Jerry comes to clear our plates and asks how everything was.
Somehow my Daddy answers saying it was all great and thanking him again.
Jerry tells him anything he can do to help he will and that my dad is a top bloke.

And then he turns to me.
'*And as for you, Lisa,*' he says.
'*You are turning into the most beautiful young lady. Isn't she?*' he says, turning to my Dad.
'*I don't know how to say this,*' he says to my Dad, '*without sounding really awful but she is really blossoming isn't she? I can't believe the change. I don't know mate, I'm just a basic guy so I can't say this the way I'm meant to nowadays, but she looks, normal.*'

Dad and I freeze and then look at each other and start laughing.
'*I've never been so insulted in my life,*' I say to Jerry.
And Daddy and I laugh and laugh.